ALFIE

All About Alfie

For Tom, with love

Other titles in the Alfie series:

Alfie Gets in First

Alfie's Feet

Alfie Gives a Hand

An Evening at Alfie's

Alfie and the Birthday Surprise

Alfie Wins a Prize

Alfie and the Big Boys

Alfie Weather

Alfie's World

Annie Rose is my Little Sister

Rhymes for Annie Rose

The Big Alfie and Annie Rose Storybook

The Big Alfie Out of Doors Storybook

ALL ABOUT ALFIE
A BODLEY HEAD BOOK 978 0 370 33194 2

Published in Great Britain by The Bodley Head,
an imprint of Random House Children's Books
A Random House Group Company

This edition published 2011

1 3 5 7 9 10 8 6 4 2

Copyright © Shirley Hughes, 2011

The right of Shirley Hughes to be identified as the author of this work has been asserted in accordance with the
Copyright, Designs and Patents Act 1988.

All rights reserved.

RANDOM HOUSE CHILDREN'S BOOKS
61–63 Uxbridge Road, London W5 5SA

www.kidsatrandomhouse.co.uk
www.alfiebooks.co.uk

Addresses for companies within The Random House Group Limited can be found at: www.randomhouse.co.uk/offices.htm

THE RANDOM HOUSE GROUP Limited Reg. No. 954009

A CIP catalogue record for this book is available from the British Library.

Printed and bound in China

ALFIE

All About Alfie

Shirley Hughes

THE BODLEY HEAD

LONDON

Where's Alfie?

Where's Alfie?
Nobody knows.
Annie Rose is calling him.
She wants him to play with her.
But there's no answer.
Because Alfie's in his secret den
At the bottom of the garden.
He's in there among the leaves
Where nobody can see him.
Not answering when he is called.
Flumbo is in there with him.
They've got provisions: a sandwich,
    a bottle of orange juice and three biscuits.
That should last for a bit.
They're planning to be a secret gang one day,
    like Robin Hood and his outlaws living in the forest.
But in the meantime, Alfie's got some special things
    in there, which nobody knows about.
There's an old key that he found in the ground,
And a precious piece of china with a blue and white pattern on it,
And a little plastic teddy.
Alfie keeps them under some leaves, where nobody can find them.
Because this is his special place.
It's his secret den.
He could even stay out here all night if he felt like it.
Well, until bedtime anyway.

The Very Special Birthday

Alfie had plenty of friends at nursery school, but his best friend was Bernard. They often played together after school. Bernard had a huge collection of cars and trucks and aeroplanes. When Alfie came to play at his house, they got them all out and raced them across the floor.

Bernard didn't have a special cuddly toy that he liked as much as Alfie liked his dear old knitted elephant, Flumbo. Usually Bernard took his favourite racing car to bed with him.

For his birthday, Alfie had given Bernard a book full of pictures
of aeroplanes, which he liked a lot. He knew the names of most of
them, even the old-fashioned ones. He had seen them in a museum.

One day Bernard came to play at Alfie's house and he brought his aeroplane book with him. After they had looked at it for a while, Mum asked them if they would like to help her ice a cake for another very special birthday. It was for Alfie's Great-Grandma Hilary.

Mum told them that she was ninety years old today, and that was very old indeed.

Alfie and Bernard helped Mum to spread the chocolate icing on the cake and make it smooth. Then they put nine candles on it (one for every ten years), and wrote a big '90' in the middle in tiny jelly sweets.

Mum said that after lunch they were going to drive to the home where Great-Grandma Hilary lived with some other elderly ladies and gentleman, and she asked Bernard if he would like to come too.

Alfie did not think that this sounded like a very interesting plan. He thought it would be much nicer to stay at home and play with Bernard. But Bernard thought it was an excellent idea. He had never met a great-grandma before and he wanted to see what she looked like. He imagined she would be very big, perhaps even a giant.

So while Mum was wrapping up Great-Grandma Hilary's present of a beautiful silk scarf, Alfie and Bernard made birthday cards for her. Alfie drew a cake on his and put a big '90' on it in coloured dots. Bernard drew a huge lady with two tiny people standing next to her, who were himself and Alfie.

After lunch, Mum put Great-Grandma Hilary's cake and present and a bunch of flowers into the car, along with Annie Rose, and they all set out. Bernard brought his aeroplane book and Alfie took Flumbo.

When they arrived, they were shown into a room where everyone was sitting, and there was Great-Grandma Hilary in a big armchair. Bernard was very surprised when he saw her, because she was not huge at all! She was a very small lady. But she smiled a big smile when she saw them.

She was very pleased with all the things they had brought, especially Alfie and Bernard's cards.

When the candles on the cake were lit and everyone in the room had sung "Happy Birthday", Great-Grandma Hilary asked Bernard and Alfie if they would help her blow them out. She thought she might not have enough puff to do it on her own.

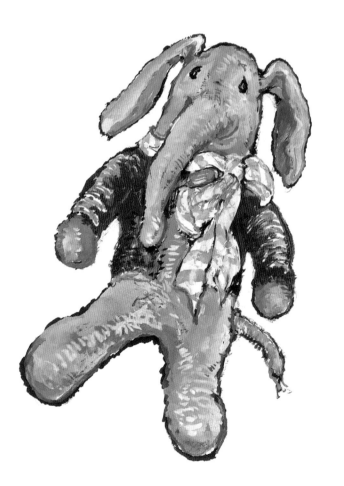

After tea, she gave Alfie the beautiful silver ribbon which Mum had used to tie up her present and helped him to make a bow around Flumbo's neck. Then she asked Bernard if he would kindly show her his aeroplane book. Bernard was even more surprised when they went through it together and she knew the names of all the old-fashioned planes.

She told Bernard that when she was young she had worked in a factory where they had actually made aeroplanes. She knew a lot about what kind of engines they had. And once she had been to an airfield and seen the pilots take off and do stunts in the sky, looping the loop and diving over the control tower.

When it was time to say goodbye, Mum and Alfie and Annie Rose gave Great-Grandma Hilary a big hug. Then it was Alfie's turn to be surprised, because Bernard gave Great-Grandma Hilary a big hug too. And hugging people was something that Bernard did not often do.

When they got back home, Alfie and Bernard both ran about with their arms spread wide, making loud aeroplane noises. They ran all over the living room and the hall, and down the passage and around the kitchen table, until at last they were so tired that they made a crash landing on the floor. It had been a very special day.

Goose Weather

Snow!
White flakes, floating and falling,
Blotting out windows,
Covering rooftops and cars and gardens,
Feathery light.
Somewhere up there,
Above the over-stuffed clouds,
Muffled in mist,
The Snow Goose is taking flight.

Alfie's Big Adventure

Alfie and Mum and Flumbo were going on a big adventure. Alfie had packed his night things and his favourite book and his special blanket. They were going to drive into the country with Mum's friend Helen and stay for two whole nights in a little cottage. There would be no other houses, only trees and fields with cows and sheep in them.

Dad and Annie Rose were staying behind. Helen was at work all day, so it was already bedtime and Alfie was in his pyjamas and dressing gown when she came to collect them. Dad and Annie Rose were on the doorstep to see them off.

Alfie and Flumbo were tucked up in the back of the car, and Mum and Helen were in the front. It was very exciting driving at night, with all the street lights on and curtains drawn and people going to bed. Alfie did not want to go to sleep. He wanted to stay awake and see everything.

Soon they were on the motorway, with big cars and trucks swooping past, and notices which Alfie could not read, and tall lampposts marching towards them one after another.

After a very long time they got onto a smaller road, and the houses got further and further apart, with fences and hedges and fields in between. Alfie was nearly asleep when the car began to bump over a rough track and through a farmyard. Then, at last, they stopped.

"Well, here we are," said Helen. They all got out of the car and stretched their stiff legs. It was absolutely, completely dark. Not like the night-time at home, with lights everywhere, but quite black all around. And very, very quiet.

Alfie held onto Flumbo very tightly in case he was frightened. In front of them was the dark shape of a little cottage, all by itself behind a wooden fence like a house in a storybook.

Helen had the key to the front door. Mum shone the big torch while Helen opened it.

They all stepped inside. There was a fusty, woody smell. Mum held the torch high. Shadows leaped against the wall.

"This is the living room," said Helen. "And the kitchen is in here. I'll just go in and turn the electricity on, so we can have a hot drink before we unpack and make up the beds."

She went over to the kitchen door. Just as she opened it, there was a noise from inside. It was a wild, fluttering, blundering noise. Then a piece of china fell on the floor and smashed. Something or somebody was inside the kitchen!

Mum dropped the torch. Helen slammed the door shut very quickly.
Then they all shot out of the cottage and stood in the garden, holding
each other's hands very tightly.

"It's all right," said Helen, in a brave voice. "It doesn't sound like a person in there, and it's certainly not a ghost. I think some creature has got in by mistake and it's just as frightened as we are."

She led the way back into the cottage. Mum and Alfie followed. Mum picked up the torch. It was still working. Then Helen opened the kitchen door, just a crack this time, very gently.

They all peered inside.

There, perched on the back of a chair, they saw an owl. It turned its head round and stared at them with big, shining eyes. Its steady gaze made it look more like a person than a bird.

Helen quietly closed the kitchen door and had a think. "It must have come down the chimney," she said. "We mustn't frighten it, but we've got to let it out somehow, and the kitchen window won't open wide enough."

So Mum ran to help her open the living-room windows and the front door. Helen picked up the tablecloth. She opened the kitchen door again, and slowly, slowly they began to edge inside.

Helen crept forward. The owl shifted its feet uneasily. Just as she was getting near enough to catch it, it suddenly swooped across the room. It knocked a mug onto the floor and broke a saucer. It flew around wildly, beating its wings against the ceiling.

Alfie clutched Flumbo very tightly and buried his face against Mum's legs.

Then, quite swiftly, the owl landed on the draining board near the sink and sat there, settling its feathers. Slowly, slowly Helen began to edge forward again. As quickly as she could, she threw the tablecloth over the owl and wrapped it around gently. Before it could flap about inside, she ran to the front door, stepped outside and let it loose.

Alfie and Mum were close behind her. Together they watched the owl fly straight out over the fence in one big swoop and high into a tree. They saw its shape among the branches, outlined against the night sky.

After a bit they went back into the cottage, and very soon the lights were on and they were sipping hot chocolate in front of the living-room fire.

"What an adventure this has turned out to be," said Mum.

"We'll clear up tomorrow morning," said Helen.

Alfie was too sleepy to say anything.

At last he and Mum and Flumbo were tucked up together in a big double bed. Just before Alfie went to sleep, he heard the owl calling from its branch under the stars. It was a lonely sound, but a nice one too.

Next morning they came down late to find Helen cooking breakfast in a clean, tidy kitchen. Alfie ate his egg and bacon sitting on the doorstep in the sunshine. Some little birds came hopping around looking for crumbs.

"Will the owl be back again?" Alfie asked.

"I don't expect so," said Mum. "Owls usually sleep in the daytime and come out at night."

"We saw him close up, didn't we?" said Alfie.

"We did," said Mum. "And I don't know who was most frightened, him or us."

"Flumbo wasn't frightened, were you, Flumbo?" said Alfie.

But Flumbo said nothing.

"We were very brave, weren't we, Mum?" said Alfie.

"We certainly were," said Mum. "*What* an adventure!"